Twinkle, Twinkle, Little Star

Jane Cabrera

To Paula,
Thanks for all your help making my books over the years.
Much love, J.C.

This edition published by Parragon Books Ltd in 2014

Parragon Books Ltd
Chartist House
15–17 Trim Street
Bath BA1 1HA, UK
www.parragon.com

Published by arrangement with Gullane Children's Books

Text © Jane Cabrera 2013
Illustrations © Jane Cabrera 2013
Based on the original poem by Jane Taylor

ISBN 978-1-4723-4295-9

Printed in China

Twinkle, Twinkle, Little Star

Jane Cabrera

PaRragon

Bath • New York • Singapore • Hong Kong • Cologne • Delhi
Melbourne • Amsterdam • Johannesburg • Shenzhen

Twinkle, twinkle, little star,
how I wonder what you are.
Up above the world so high,
Like a diamond in the sky.

Twinkle, twinkle, little star,
how I wonder what you are.

Sparkle, sparkle, little star,
how I wonder what you are.
Peeking through the silent trees...

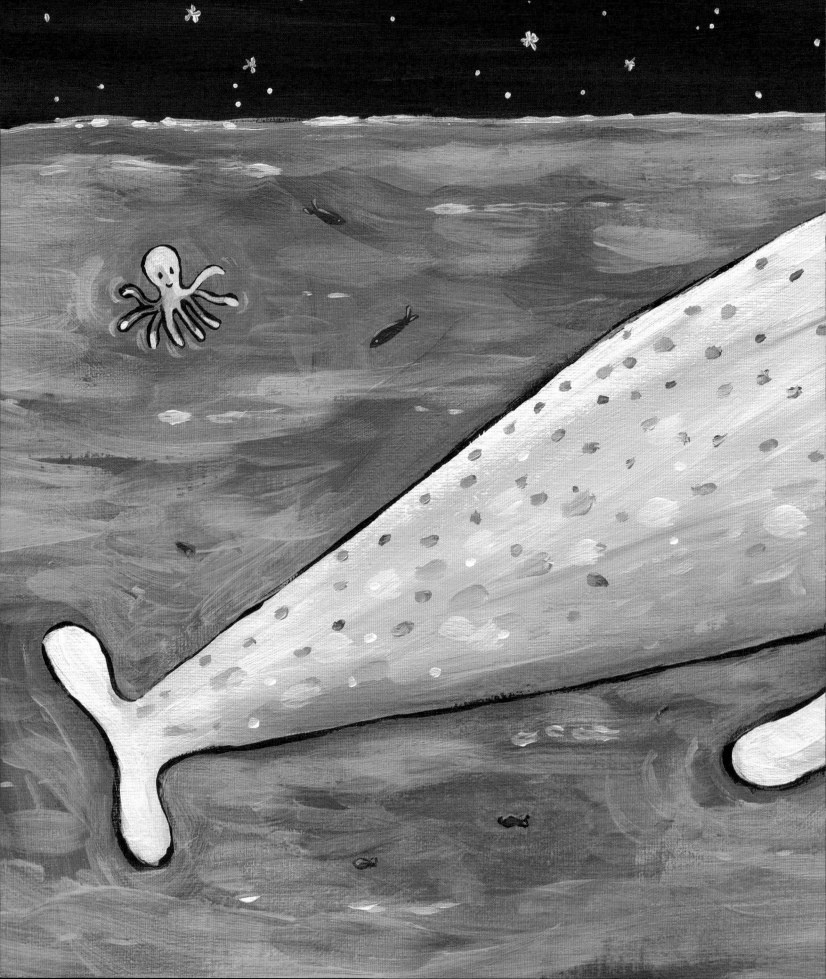

...high above the deep blue seas.
Sparkle, sparkle, little star,
how I wonder what you are.

Flicker, flicker, little star,
how I wonder what you are.
Smiling down on desert dry...

...lighting up the cold night sky.
Flicker, flicker, little star,
how I wonder what you are.

Shimmer, shimmer, little star,
how I wonder what you are.
Over zigzag roofs so high ...

...where the mountain meets the sky.
Shimmer, shimmer, little star,
how I wonder what you are.

Glisten, glisten, little star,
how I wonder what you are.
Up above the grassy plain...

...through the warm, wet jungle rain.
Glisten, glisten, little star,
how I wonder what you are.

Twinkle, twinkle, little star,
the whole world wonders what you are.
Shine your twinkly magic light
over all the Earth tonight.

Twinkle over towns and trees,
fields and farms, lakes and seas.
Twinkle, twinkle, up above...

for me and for
the one I love.